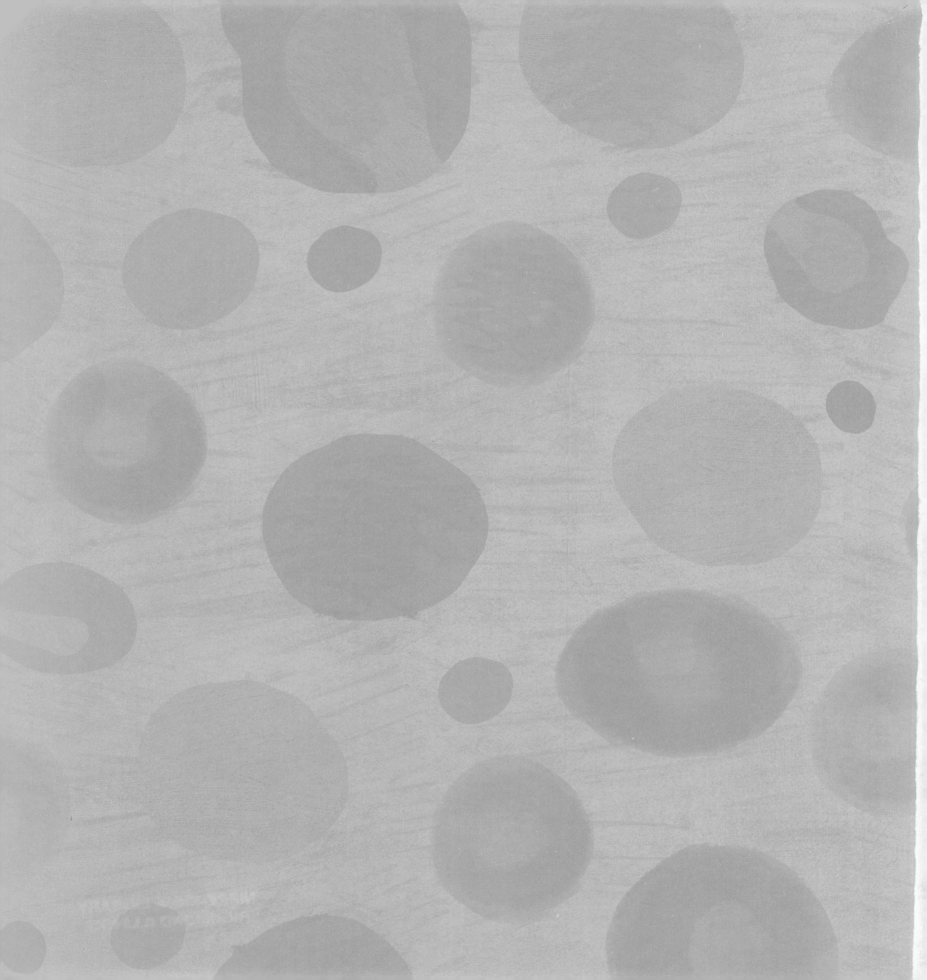

WE SHALL NOT CEASE FROM EXPLORATION, AND THE END OF ALL OUR EXPLORING WILL BE TO ARRIVE WHERE WE STARTED AND KNOW THE PLACE FOR THE FIRST TIME.

T. S. Eliot

TO MY HAIRY,
UNCIVILIZED FRIEND ERIN,
WITH LOVE.

First U.S. edition 2018

Library of Congress Catalog Card Number pending
ISBN 978-0-7636-9628-3

17 18 19 20 21 22 GBL 10 9 8 7 6 5 4 3 2 1

Printed in Shenzhen, Guangdong, China

This book was typeset in Edbaskerville.
The illustrations were created digitally.

Nosy Crow
an imprint of
Candlewick Press
99 Dover Street
Somerville, Massachusetts 02144

www.nosycrow.com
www.candlewick.com

DAVE'S CAVE

FRANN PRESTON-GANNON

nosy Crow™

An imprint of Candlewick Press

This Dave.

This Dave's cave.

Dave like cave.
Nice green grass.

Dave's friends
like cave, too.

But Dave **not** happy.
Dave wide awake.

Maybe Dave find **better**
cave with **greener** grass
and **bigger** rocks.

Dave want **new** cave.

Dave put out fire.

Off Dave go.

But first cave not **quite** right.

Second cave
not cozy like home.

Third cave
too noisy.

Fourth cave nice,
but Dave not like pets.

but Jon **not** like sharing.

Dave sad.

Maybe . . .

no better cave,
with greener grass
and bigger rocks.

But look! This cave nice.

Green grass.

Big rocks.

This
cave
perfect.

This cave . . .

home.